Dear Delainey

Have fun finding the hidden ladybug on each painti,
little Freddy, the stuffed animal, enclosed. ENJOY!
    Best wishes,
    Madeline Houptman, illustrator
    New York, April 2, 2015

FRIENDLY FREDDY

FREDDY

WRITTEN BY ANGELA BAVISTER
PAINTINGS BY MADELINE HAUPTMAN

WONDERFUL

PUBLISHING

NEW YORK & LONDON

FRIENDLY FREDDY

Published in the United States by Wonderful Publishing

Printed and bound in North Mankato, Minnesota, U.S.A. by Corporate Graphics
First Edition

Library of Congress Control Number: 2010928267

Hardcover: ISBN 978-0-9798421-1-5; ISBN 0-9798421-1-5

dedication

Angela Baviser, the British author who wrote **FRIENDLY FREDDY**, dedicates this book to two important family members: to Richard, her husband, who has encouraged her to pursue her love of writing; and to Oscar, her mother's adorable dachshund, who inspired the story.

Madeline Hauptman, the American artist who illustrated **FRIENDLY FREDDY**, dedicates this book to her mother, who started her doing artwork at an early age; to her husband, Allen, who inspires her to paint; and to her children, Dan, Marissa, and Nicole, and son-in-law, Cory, all of whom who make her smile. Special thanks to Charlie, Nicole and Cory's dog, who graciously taste-tested and loved the homemade peanut butter dog biscuits.

Angela and Madeline jointly dedicate this book to Mamma Agata. If not for her very wonderful cookery course on the Amalfi Coast of Italy, which is where the author and artist met, this delightful transatlantic collaboration would never have happened!

The paintings in this book were inspired, in part, by Stone Barns Center for Food and Agriculture, a nonprofit farm and education center in Pocantico Hills, New York, that has beautiful farm animals. See if you can find the hidden ladybug (🐞) on each painting!

FREDDY is a black and tan dachshund, also known as a **sausage** dog. He is little, with a long body, short legs, and a shiny coat.

FREDDY is a very **cheerful** dog. He loves making new friends, and he always thinks everybody will be pleased to meet him. When he meets a new friend, his tail starts wagging, his ears go back to show he is smiling and he bounces around in **excitement**.

FREDDY and his family have just moved to a farm in the country. It is winter, the trees are bare and there is frost on the ground.

sausage - a shape that is long and thin   **cheerful -** happy   **excitement** - joy

On his first day on the farm FREDDY decides to explore.

It is very cold outside, but FREDDY is warm because he is wearing a **snug** wool jacket. He is having a good sniff around, when he comes across a chicken **hutch.** He opens the small side door and peeks inside.

snug - warm and comfortable   **hutch** - a large cage for small animals

6

Inside the hutch
FREDDY sees
three chickens
resting peacefully.

Immediately his tail starts wagging, his ears go back and he starts bouncing around. "Hello!" he woofs. "I'm FREDDY. I've just moved here. What are your names?"

The chickens look at him rather **suspiciously**. Then one of them **clucks**, "I'm Maggie and these are my sisters, Annie and Betty. What sort of a dog are you?"

"I'm a sausage dog," barks FREDDY. "I may be little with short legs but I've got lots of energy and I love making new friends – so I'm very pleased to meet you!" The three chickens all cluck together, "We're pleased to meet you, too!" Maggie says, "Come and visit us whenever you like."

FREDDY is **delighted** to have made friends with Maggie, Annie and Betty, the three chickens.

suspiciously - with distrust or doubt   **clucks** - makes the sound of a chicken
delighted - very pleased

He sets off on his way and comes to a frozen pond with some ducks sitting on the grass by the edge. It is extremely cold outside, but the ducks have lots of fluffy feathers to keep them warm. When **FREDDY** sees the ducks, his tail starts wagging, his ears go back and he starts bouncing around in excitement. "Hello!" he woofs, "I'm **FREDDY**. I've just moved here and I've met Maggie and her sisters. What are your names?"

The ducks look at him rather nervously. Then the one with orange on his face quacks, "I'm Eddie and these are my friends, Tom, Jim and Dan. We don't like dogs that chase us so I hope you are not that kind of dog."

"Not at all," answers **FREDDY**. "I'm a very friendly sausage dog and I would never chase ducks. I like making new friends – so I'm very pleased to meet you!"

The ducks look **relieved** and they all quack together, "It's nice to meet you, **FREDDY** – come and say hello whenever you're passing the pond!"

relieved - less worried

FREDDY runs
off happily on
his little legs,
thrilled to have
made friends
with the ducks.
He continues on
his way, towards
the large stone barn.

While he is wondering what sort of animals might live in the barn, suddenly two **lumbering** cows appear. They **plod** towards FREDDY and then stand still, staring at him silently.

FREDDY feels rather unsure of himself as the cows are quite large and look a little **frightening**. But he **plucks** up his courage, his tail starts wagging slightly and he puts his ears back a little. Then he barks, "Hello, I'm FREDDY."

The cows simply continue to stare at him blankly. FREDDY feels a bit uncomfortable and wonders whether perhaps making friends with the chickens and ducks was enough for one day. Just as he is about to turn around and leave, feeling rather **disheartened**, one of the cows moos, "Hello, I'm Sally, and this is Polly. We're not used to other animals being friendly to us."

FREDDY is delighted that the cows have responded. He starts wagging his tail, putting his ears back and bouncing around in excitement. "I'm very pleased to meet you," he woofs. "I'm a very friendly sausage dog and I love meeting all kinds of animals." The cows moo, "We're pleased to be friends with you, FREDDY! Come and visit whenever you like."

---

lumbering - moving in a slow and heavy way   **plod** - walk slowly
frightening - scary   **plucks** - gathers   **disheartened** - very sad

FREDDY is feeling very pleased with himself at having made so many friends in one day! What a good start to his new life on the farm!

He continues on his tour of the farm and comes to a **frosty** field where he sees a rather **dejected**-looking donkey. The donkey has a long face and rather **shabby,** light brown fur.

frosty - very cold   **dejected** - sad   **shabby** - old and worn thin

FREDDY starts wagging his tail, putting his ears back and bouncing around in excitement. "Hello there!" FREDDY barks up at the donkey. "I'm FREDDY and I've just moved here. I've made friends with the chickens, the ducks, and the cows and now I thought I would say hello to you!"

The donkey **glares** at FREDDY, and does not answer. FREDDY thinks perhaps the donkey is a bit deaf. "HELLO!" he woofs again. "I'm not sure if you heard me **properly**, but I'm FREDDY!"

The donkey does not even look at FREDDY this time, but turns around and walks away and FREDDY feels sad.

glares - stares at with anger   **properly** - correctly

FREDDY is very **despondent**. He doesn't understand why the donkey doesn't want to be friends with him.

FREDDY goes back to the house, eats a homemade peanut butter dog biscuit*, then sits down in front of the fireplace, **pondering** over his strange **encounter** with the donkey.

despondent - having lost hope   **pondering** - thinking carefully   **encounter -** meeting

* homemade peanut butter dog biscuit recipe is on page 32

The next day, **FREDDY** decides to investigate the donkey problem. He goes to see the chickens and the ducks, and asks them each about the donkey in the field. They tell him that the donkey is named Hector, and that he is the **grumpiest** donkey in the world.

FREDDY then goes to see the cows, and asks them, "What do you know about Hector?" Sally moos, "He's always miserable – don't bother trying to make friends with him. He's very old now but his age is no excuse for him to be so **bad-tempered**. And for some reason, he's always worse in winter."

FREDDY thinks about everything he has heard. He can't understand why the donkey could be so unfriendly. **FREDDY** decides that something must be making Hector unhappy. **FREDDY** is puzzled over what Sally said about Hector being more bad-tempered in winter.

Suddenly, the answer comes to **FREDDY**. It is bitterly cold but there is no shelter in Hector's field and nothing to keep him warm. The chickens have a little hutch. The ducks have their warm, fluffy feathers. The cows have their barn. But poor old Hector has only a shabby coat of fur that is thinning **dreadfully**, and no **shelter** at all.

Poor Hector is cold and that's what makes him so grumpy!

---

grumpiest - most easily annoyed   **bad-tempered** - angry, cross   **dreadfully** - very badly
shelter - a place that gives protection

FREDDY rushes to his bed, and grabs one end of his thick, warm, blue blanket with his teeth. He drags the large blanket through the house, outside into the garden and runs on the path that winds through the farm.

The chickens, ducks and cows all look at FREDDY in **astonishment** as he runs past them dragging a blanket.

FREDDY continues along the path, past the stone wall, until he reaches the field where Hector lives.

astonishment - great surprise

FREDDY puts down the blanket and barks up at Hector, "I thought you must be cold with no coat and no shelter so I've brought you this blanket."

Hector quickly puts on the blanket and he stares at FREDDY in surprise. Hector looks as if he doesn't quite know what to do next.

FREDDY woofs, "I've got to go now but I hope this blanket will keep you warm, Hector."

The next day, FREDDY pays Hector another visit.

"Hi Hector!" FREDDY barks cautiously. Hector looks up and FREDDY sees he is looking happy. "Hello FREDDY," Hector **brays**. "Thank you for the blanket – I haven't felt this warm in winter, for years!" Hector **hee-haws** with happiness.

FREDDY is delighted. His tail starts wagging, his ears go back to show he is smiling, and he starts bouncing around in excitement. Hector smiles with a twinkle in his eye, at having the good luck to meet this friendly little sausage dog.

Being friendly, kind and trying to understand Hector made FREDDY feel good.

FRIENDLY FREDDY learned that when you bring happiness to others, you also bring happiness to yourself.

brays or **hee-haws** - makes the loud, harsh sound of a donkey

FRIENDLY FREDDY'S HEALTHY, HOMEMADE PEANUT BUTTER DOG BISCUITS

Dogs love these biscuits, and people also enjoy them.

1)   In a bowl, mix **DRY** ingredients:
      1 cup whole wheat flour
      1/2 cup white flour
      2 teapsoons baking powder

2)   In a separate bowl (or food processor), mix **MOIST** ingredients:
      1/4 cup natural peanut butter (with no sugar or salt added)
      1 Tablespoon olive oil
      1 egg
      1/4 cup water

3)   Then add **DRY** ingredients to **MOIST** ingredients to form a ball of dough. (You may need to add 1 Tablespoon more water to form ball.) Roll out dough to 1/4 inch thickness. With cookie cutters, cut biscuits into shapes and place biscuits on greased cookie sheet.

4)   Bake for 20 minutes at 325º F (162° C, Gas Mark 3). Turn off oven, then leave biscuits in oven 20 minutes more, so they get nice and crisp.

ALLERGEN INFORMATION: Recipe for biscuits includes products that contain peanuts. Publisher is not responsible or liable if any persons or animals are allergic to or harmed by biscuits made according to the above Healthy, Homemade Peanut Butter Dog Biscuits Recipe.